The Cooley Girls

by Brad Stephens

Baker's Plays
7611 Sunset Blvd.
Los Angeles, CA 90042
BAKERSPLAYS.COM

THE COOLEY GIRLS was produced by The Lancaster Players on November 8, 2007 in White Stone, Virginia. The production was directed by John Baumhardt, with set design by Janice Stewart. The cast was as follows:

ROSE.....................................Susan Robertson

MARGARET BOWLING...........................Kinnet Ehring

ESTER...Robin Blake

BRENDA...Tess Dumais

HARRIET......................................Sharon Robertson

JEFFREY.......................................Miracle Gordon

THE CHARACTERS
(in order of appearance)

ROSE – The youngest sister
MARGARET BOWLING – Rose's neighbor
ESTER – Harriet's daughter
BRENDA – The middle sister
HARRIET – The eldest sister
JEFFREY – Brenda's husband

THE TIME
The present.

Act I
February of the present.

Act II
Scene 1 - Four months later.
Scene 2 - Two days later.

ACT ONE

Scene One

*(**SETTING**: The play is set in Muncie, Indiana. The time is the present.)*

(The stage is dark as the action begins. Small spots above the stage area light when each sequence of action begins, bathing the scene below in round pools of light.)

*(**AT RISE**: Light cue. Downstage left light comes up, revealing an auburn haired woman in her late forties standing at the sink washing dishes. She is **ROSE COOLEY**. She wears a full apron, yellow rubber gloves and hanging about her neck on a beaded chain is a pair of glasses. The sink is mounted on a wheeled cabinet base. Next to the cabinet unit sits a stool, on the stool sits **ROSE**'s neighbor, **MARGARET BOWLING**. They are talking as the action begins.)*

ROSE. A reunion you say…Oh, Margaret, that's sounds like a wonderful idea, I love reunions.

MARGARET. Well, it's not really a reunion Rose, you know…more of a get-together I'd guess you'd call it, just my sister and her two children from Atlanta and my brother, Fred, of course. I told you about him didn't I…the engineer. He lives in Indianapolis. I just thought it would be a good idea for all of us to get together again, catch up on the family news, things like that. You know we haven't seen each other since last Christmas…My and how my sister's girls have grown. They're five and seven now you know and so pretty…so well behaved and polite.

*(leans into **ROSE**)*

Did you know that they call me…Auntie Marg…isn't that cute, Auntie Marg?

ROSE. *(She looks up as if lost in thought.)* A reunion...my what a nice thing Margaret...

MARGARET. *(turns to her)* Rose...how silly of me...here I am barging in on you like this to borrow your Jell-o mold and...well...I nearly forgot...why don't you join us, you know for the reunion. I don't know why I didn't think of it before this. It's nothing fancy mind you, just family. And...well since your Henry has passed on... your being alone and all like you are...oh, please say yes. Please, Rose?

ROSE. Oh, Margaret, it's dear of you to ask me but...I'd be butting in, really I would. It's your family after all...I'd feel like a fifth wheel...I would.

MARGARET. Nonsense...Now, Rose, that's just nonsense, please don't say no,

(She has a thought.)

Wait, I just thought of something, since you don't have a family...you can be part of ours, now, how's that? Part of our family, wouldn't that be nice?

ROSE. *(stops washing dishes and looks at her)* That's sweet of you Margaret, but you see I do have family.

(pause)

Really I do...well, two sisters that is, but they are my family.

MARGARET. *(a bit surprised)* You do?...Two sisters. Why I've never heard you mention them, not once and I've been your next-door neighbor for...well, since before your Henry died. You never said you had sisters.

ROSE. Well I do, Margaret. Their names are Harriet and Brenda...those are their names...Harriet and Brenda Cooley.

MARGARET. *(shocked)* My goodness, what a surprise! And all this time I thought you had no one, no family at all... Well, where are they, what do they do...how old are they...are they married...do they have any children?

ROSE. *(a long embarrassed pause before the truth comes out)* I don't know.

MARGARET. *(surprised)* You…you don't know. What do you mean you don't know? But you just said you had two sisters. You must know something about them…Don't they keep in touch with you?

ROSE. I…that is we…

(pause as she thinks how to tell her)

Well, Margaret you see the fact of the matter is I haven't seen my sisters in years. I don't even know where they live or if they are still alive…When we were just young-sters we were all put up for adoption…and that was so many years ago…We just lost track of each other.

MARGARET. *(shocked)* Adoption…Rose, how terrible for you and for your sisters…adoption…not to know…What an awful thing to happen to you all…How long has it been since, since you've seen each other, spoken to one another?

ROSE. *(looks off for a beat)* Too long I'm afraid, much too long…since we were…well, youngsters, I know that. It's been a long time though. I was just eight and Brenda was, well, let me see…she would have been fifteen and Harriet, she was the oldest she had to be seventeen.

MARGARET. Well, how many years has it been Rose?

ROSE. Come October it will be forty years.

MARGARET. Did you say forty years, Rose!

(She thinks about this.)

That's, that's almost half a lifetime…Do you know that…half a lifetime.

ROSE. I know.

(She nods.)

I know.

MARGARET. Did your parents die or something like that, I mean for you all be put up for adoption.

ROSE. No, nothing like that…you see my Father…my Father just left us, just packed up and left us, and then my Mother….Well, this is terrible to say I know…but she…she had this very good job offer in San Diego…

MARGARET. Rose, what are you telling me…what are you saying? That your Mother and Father just abandoned you youngsters like that?…Just like that.

ROSE. No, Margaret…it was…well I supposed Father just wanted more from life, more than he found at home I guess.

(looks off)

I don't think he was ever happy there…never truly happy at home…that's why he left. And as I said, Mother was offered this wonderful job in California, oh she was going to send for us in time, she told us that, really she did…you know once she got settled.

MARGARET. And did she…send for you all?

ROSE. Well…no.

MARGARET. Rose…

(rises and puts her arms around her and holds her)

Oh, my poor Rose, what an awful thing to have happen to you and your sisters…to be well, to be just left like that.

ROSE. Well, I suppose they had their reasons, Margaret… but her sister did raise us for a while…so I guess you could say we weren't really alone.

MARGARET. Her sister? Her sister raised you then…Well surely she would know where your sisters would be wouldn't she?

ROSE. No…no I don't think she would.

MARGARET. *(shaking her head)* And so in all this time you've not seen your…You've never heard from them…not even a phone call, a card…not to see or speak to your sisters and in all those years… Didn't you ever try to find them?

ROSE. I tried once, it must have been about ten years ago… but…well, it seems that adoption records like that are sealed…did you know that, Margaret…They are… sealed by the court you know, no one can see them… That's what I was told, that it was the law.

MARGARET. *(some insistence in her voice)* Well, you should try again…really you should Rose, you should just try again…I know that if I had two sisters that I hadn't seen in forty years, well I can tell you that I would certainly try again… Keeping me from finding them just because of some silly law…well I would just try again.

ROSE. Do you really think I should? They did tell me that, about it being the law.

MARGARET. Of course I do… You just put your foot down and fight Rose, fight them…keeping you separated from your sisters just because of some silly law…

(She looks at **ROSE.** *)*

Oh, Rose, now look what I've done… I've probably upset you, I'm sorry… I should never have asked you to go into all of this. Really I shouldn't have. To make you…well, to bring all of this up.

(She stands and looks around feeling slightly guilty for having made **ROSE** *recall her past.)*

Look, Rose…I do have to be going… I'll just get the mold on my way out… Now don't forget you are going to join us, now that's a promise.

(gives **ROSE** *a hug)*

Goodbye…and…

(She pauses and gives **ROSE** *another hug.)*

We love you, Rose.

(She turns and begins to exit shaking her head.)

Forty years.

(She exits as **ROSE** *still stands at the sink. She then speaks softly, almost in a dream like tone.)*

ROSE. Yes…yes…I'll be there and thank you for the invite… A reunion…what a lovely idea…

(She stands at the sink as the light above her slowly fades to black.)

Scene Two

(Light cue)

(Stage right spot comes up.)

*(It is now months later. Stage right a woman sits at a small phone table. It is **ROSE COOLEY**. She is dressed in a simple housedress minus the apron and without the rubber gloves from before. Her glasses now perch on her nose. In front of her on the table sits a phone along with several stacks of loose papers and several spiral note pads. As the lights cue on we see she in on the phone talking. Action begins.)*

ROSE. Good afternoon, this is Rose Cooley Warren calling. I hope you won't think me silly, but I am trying to contact my sister…that's right my sister…her name is Harriet Cooley, Harriet Cooley Smith and this was the number I was given. Is Mrs. Smith there?…Oh, I see… this is Mrs. Smith. Well as I said I hope this isn't an imposition, but I am trying to contact my sister, Harriet, would you happen to be her?

(She nods her head.)

I see…oh…you've never had a sister… only a brother… Raymond.

(pause)

Oh, he does, how nice…Madison, Wisconsin, you say…Ah, Mrs. Smith, may I ask you one last question before you hang up…did your people happen to come from Ohio…Lebanon, Ohio to be exact…No…Little Rock…

(She nods again.)

I see. Well I am sorry to have bothered you then and thank you for your time…yes, and you too.

(She hangs up and then with care crosses the name from her list. Then running her finger down the page she stops, picks up the phone and dials another number. As the phone begins to ring another spotlight at stage left comes on.)

Scene Three

(Light cue)

(This light cue reveals a large comfortable sofa. On the sofa we see sleeping the figure of a woman with auburn hair dressed in slacks and a large T-shirt with the words, God Is The Answer, *printed across the front of it. She quietly snores. She is in her mid-fifties, a Bible lies on her stomach. Again the phone rings. Finally, a woman enters stage left. She is in her late twenties with auburn hair held away from her face by a large brimmed sun hat. It is obvious that she is unhappy that it is she who has to answer the phone. As she passes the figure on the sofa she gives her a disgusted glance. The woman wears a tight fitting bathing suit and dark glasses. She chews gum. She walks to the phone and answers it.)*

ESTER. Brandy…Brandy, if this is you girl, you are in deep doo-doo I'll tell you that right now…dragging me in here like this. I just hope to hell that this is a *real* important call, girl.

(She pulls down her sun glasses and glances at one of her arms.)

Cause you see I've just been lying out there in that damn hot broiling sun, being burnt to a crisp for the last twenty-five minutes trying to keep up this tan here of mine before my big date tonight and I had only five more minutes left before I had to turn over on my tummy…

ROSE. Oh…I am sorry to have bothered you then, but this…

ESTER. You're not Brandy…who is this?

ROSE. No…no, I'm not I'm afraid, as I said this is Rose Cooley Warren calling from Muncie, you know… Muncie, Indiana. I was looking for a Harriet Cooley, Harriet Cooley Smith. Have I reached the right number?

ESTER. Yes…

(She looks at the figure on of sofa.)

ESTER. *(cont.)* Harriet Smith lives here...so...why are you calling? Who'd you say you were again?

ROSE. I said, I'm Rose Cooley Warren. I am Harriet's sister...at least I hope I have the right Harriet Smith... And who are you?

ESTER. I'm her daughter, Ester...So who is this again?

ROSE. Her daughter? Her daughter did you say...Oh, gracious then you, then you must be...my niece!...Oh, good heavens then I...I'm your Aunt...It's your mother's sister, your Aunt Rose calling...

ESTER. *(She nods her head sure the call is a prank.)* I see...Say what is this a joke...some kind of game show?...

ROSE. A game show?

ESTER. Yeah, you know like...*This Is Your Life*...where they have some weird stranger from your past come out and...

ROSE. Oh, no it's nothing like that... It's nothing at all like that at all. You see we...well, that is me and my two sisters have not seen each other in forty years and... well...oh my...I do have the right Harriet Smith, don't I?

ESTER. Beats me...I've never heard her mention anything about having any sisters...Look, are you sure you got the right number?

ROSE. Well, as I said, I'm not sure, not sure at all. I was given a list of names and telephone numbers by the Ohio Office of Social Services to call and this was one of the numbers listed for Harriet Smith.

ESTER. Social Services you said...Now just hold your horses here, what's this all about?

ROSE. Yes...but surely your mother must have told you...

ESTER. Told me...told me what?... Look here who ever you are, you're beginning to confuse me now...

ROSE. Why...that she, that is that we...that we three children were put up for adoption back in Ohio almost forty years ago...that's why I am trying to contact her.

ESTER. Adoption!...Well, I'll be...you mean that my... adopted...

ROSE. But I thought you knew...that she had a sister...Oh, I am sorry.

ESTER. No problem. The way my life's been going lately it sure as hell won't be my first surprise...Probably not my last one either... So you say she might be your sister.

ROSE. Well I hope so, is she there? I would like to talk to...

ESTER. Hold on here a minute...Let's not rush things. How do I know this is not some kind of scam...you know... it happens all the time...one of those telephone con jobs...

(She removes her sunglasses as she thinks for several beats.)

What does she look like, this sister of yours, you know the one you lost, the one you haven't seen in...what was it forty-years ago...describe her.

ROSE. Oh my, describe her you said...

*(**ROSE** fidgets with the phone cord as she tries to remember.)*

I...she...I...well, I don't know. That is I don't know what she looks like today, but when we were girls she was...well, let me see....She was about five feet tall, maybe a little taller you know, but, well I'm sure she's grown by now...and...oh yes, she lost a front tooth, does that help...her middle one...

*(**ESTER LOU** looks at the sleeping figure and slowly parts her lips to looks then shakes her head.)*

That I do remember, she lost her front tooth when she fell off of her bicycle...and let me see...she had red hair...auburn hair actually. Well all of us girls had auburn hair just like our mother's side of the family...

ESTER. *(looks down again at the sleeping woman and nods)* Auburn hair...ok...I'll give you that one...what else?

ROSE. *(now thinking)* What else...now just let me think for a minute it's been so long ago...Just give me a minute...

ESTER. Just you go right ahead and take your time, take all the time you need here Rosy...

ROSE. Thank you...oh...her toe, that's it, her little toe.

ESTER. Her what?

ROSE. I said her toe, her little toe on her...

(**ROSE** *tries to think which toe.*)

Her left foot I think it was. When she was eleven she cut it on rock...or was it a piece of glass...no...a rock, I'm sure it was a rock. She has a scar. A tiny little scar that looks like a half moon...

(*She draws it in the air with her finger.*)

You know a little curvy thing.

ESTER. I see...a little *curvy* thing.

(*She now walks to the feet of the woman on the sofa and closely inspects her right foot before finding what she is looking for.*)

Well, damn it, Rose, I think you just hit the daily double, I think you just found your sister, Harriet...

(*All lights go to black.*)

Scene Four

(Cue as lights again come up on **ROSE.***)*

*(***ROSE** *is still sitting at the phone table. She is dialing the phone again. Once more we hear it ring. After several more rings a spot light comes up center stage, we see a wing chair. Just to the right of the chair sits a floor lamp. A phone sits on a small table to the right of the lamp. A women enters. She wears blue jeans and a large man's shirt, which hangs over her jeans. Her auburn hair sticks out wildly from her head, a headband holds it back from her forehead. Heavy loop earrings dangle from her ears. She reaches for the phone as she flops into the chair.)*

BRENDA. I've got it Jeffrey…Hello…Give peace a chance.

ROSE. And…hello to you. This is Mrs. Rose Cooley Warren calling, I hate to bother you like this, but I am trying to track down my sister, Brenda Cooley Chatsworth. Is Mrs. Chatsworth there please?

(a long silence)

BRENDA. *(surprise)* Who did you just say?

ROSE. *(slower)* Brenda Cooley Chatsworth.

BRENDA. No…

(slowly as if considering her response)

No, I heard that part. I mean before that…the part when you said who was calling?

ROSE. Oh yes…this is Rose Cooley. Rose Marie Cooley.

BRENDA. *(a look of shock comes over her)* Did you say Rose Cooley?

(She thinks for a moment.)

R-o-s-e M-a-r-i-e C-o-o-l-e-y…I had a sister once named that, named Rose Cooley, but that was…hell, that was years ago…

(concern in her voice now)

Who did you say this was? Where did you say you were calling from?… Now what's this all about?

ROSE. *(all aflutter now she begins to speak)* You mean this is you, Brenda...oh, oh good gracious...I can't believe it...yes it's me...Rose...your sister, Rose, calling you all the way from Muncie, Indiana...I can't believe I found you. Oh, I think I'm going to cry...Brenda, is this really you?

BRENDA. Rose?...My God it is you. I still remember that voice of yours.

ROSE. Brenda, then it really is you?

BRENDA. Yes, Rose I'm afraid it must be me. Now how in God's name did you ever find me, Rose, it's been...

(She mentally counts.)

What...how many years ago... And just why are you calling?

ROSE. Forty years next October, October the twenty-first to be exact...I know it has been a long time hasn't it?

BRENDA. My God, you even remember the date? Then you must be Rose, only Rose Cooley would remember that date.

ROSE. Yes, it was October the twenty-first, it rained that day remember...oh, Brenda, it is you and after all of this time. How are you?... I have so many questions to ask you... Oh, Brenda, I can't believe this, that I am talking to my sister and after...

(She stands.)

Oh, I nearly forgot, guess what?

BRENDA. *(a cautious tone in her voice now)* Now what?

ROSE. *(proudly)* I have found Harriet ,too.

BRENDA. *(She stands stunned by the news.)* You found...Harriet!...Harriet! Oh good God, I don't believe this.

ROSE. What? What did you say Brenda, I didn't hear you?

BRENDA. Forget it, Rose.

ROSE. Anyway I found her, can you believe it, just today, really I did. She lives in Pula Springs, Nevada. Oh, and she has a daughter, did you know that, isn't that exciting, a dear little daughter named Ester…just think of it Brenda, I'm an Aunt…well, so are you of course…we are both Aunts… Anyway, Ester, that's her daughter, said that Harriet was resting, but she said that she would have her call me back later…can you believe it?

BRENDA. *(sits)* Rose…I asked you before…How did you find me?

ROSE. Oh…from Social Service in Ohio, they had files on all of us…did you know that, after the adoptions…it seems they kept records on you and Harriet and well on all of us…that's how I found you, through Social Services.

BRENDA. That figures, the damn government again, prying into our personal lives. Sticking their noses where they don't belong. For Godsake, there's no privacy in this country anymore…

ROSE. What did you say?

BRENDA. You heard me Rose. I said the government. Prying into our lives…

(She stands.)

You know they keep files and records on all of us didn't you, well you had to, it's common knowledge, I mean even living in a place like Muncie, Indiana you must have known all about that. Hell, they've been doing it for years…have files on everyone in the whole god damned country stored out there in some vault buried who knows how deep under some mountain out in Montana…country's nothing but one big concentration camp… Orwell come to life. Do you understand me Rose, probably listening in to this call right now…this very minute. Phone taps, hidden cameras…oh they know all the tricks…happens every day…Chertoff's Boy's never sleep Rose, never. Don't forget that…

(She holds the phone away from her face and speaks loudly.)

BRENDA. *(cont.)* Isn't that right Mr. Chertoff's Goon Squad who's probably listening in to every damn word I'm uttering here…aren't you…listening to me talk on the telephone to my sister Rose out there in Muncie, Indiana, right…well great, I just hope you are getting a real earful.

(She looks toward the phone again and speaks in a louder voice.)

Now Rose, about that *bomb* we're planning on building…

(She laughs.)

ROSE. *(a long pause)* Brenda…maybe I called at a bad time? …I can call back later if you'd like.

BRENDA. Don't worry Rose, the Gestapo probably don't have a file on you…yet.

ROSE. *(nervously)* Gestapo!…A file…did you say a file on me…Is that what you said? Brenda, why should the government have a file on me?

BRENDA. Relax, Rose, just calm down. God, you're as skittish as when you were a little girl. Now just calm down will you, I was only teasing about the bomb…not the Gestapo part…just the bomb. Now, Rose, why did you call?

ROSE. *(still dazed by talk of the Gestapo and wire taps)* Why… why did I…call?…

(For a moment she thinks.)

Oh, I almost forgot…

(She calms down.)

Now I remember. I called to, well to see if you were still…still…still around.

BRENDA. Oh, I see, you mean you called to see if I had kicked the bucket yet, isn't that it?

ROSE. *(She stands.)* Brenda, what a terrible thing to say. No, it was nothing like that…nothing at all like that… although…well we are getting older now and reaching the age when…well when things like that can happen…you know…

BRENDA. Like I said Rose, kick the bucket, you just called to see if I'd checked out yet is that it?

ROSE. Heavens no, nothing like that, I just thought if I could find you both, you and Harriet, well it would just be nice to find out what you all have been doing, about your lives…that it might be nice to meet again… you know after all of these years, just once to meet one more time…for old times sake so to speak.

BRENDA. Meet again? For old times sake?…Is that why you have tracked Harriet and me down like this after forty-years, for old times sake…Why? Just tell me that Rose, why? Why would we ever want to do that?

ROSE. I just thought it would be a nice idea that's all. I just wanted to know what you and Harriet have done in your lives. If you ever married? About your children?…Things like that you know, family things…Oh, Brenda wouldn't if be fun for just the three of us to get together again, a reunion, you know like when we were little, like before …

BRENDA. You mean like before *Mother*, adorable brain-washed *Mother* tossed us out on our fannies to be shipped off to those rotten foster homes…Is that what you mean Rose?…Well, no thank you, you can count me out.

ROSE. But Brenda, Mother couldn't help it…

BRENDA. Oh Rose, you were always so, well so damn gull-ible. You always accepted everything…Don't tell me you bought into that crap she told us…Mother…Then there was Dad…running out on her like he did…running out on us.

ROSE. He didn't run out on her or us Brenda…he went off with that other woman…from his office, you remember the one. Mother told us all about that…

BRENDA. See what I mean, Rose. Even now you believe everything she told us…Dad didn't run away with anyone but himself for Godsake, it was her, Mother, she drove him out. My God Rose, the man had no balls, he never stood up to her, you know that…not once, not ever. He yes'd her to death…She used him Rose, she never loved him, just used him. She was like one of those black widow spiders, just sucked him dry and then kicked him out. I'm telling you Rose, she never loved anyone, not him, not us, no one.

ROSE. But Brenda…

BRENDA. It was a lie, don't you understand that Rose, haven't you figured all of this out by now? Our life was never like we imagined it, every bit of it a giant conservative lie.

ROSE. *(She stands.)* Now Brenda, stop it. Just stop it. She did what she thought was right at the time for her girls… for us… And as for her not loving…

BRENDA. And that job she was offered, remember that job she kept talking about…the one that was waiting for her in San Diego…And how she couldn't take us with her until after she got settled…how she was going to send for us…so we could all start a new life in California…Do you remember that. That's when we were shipped off to that sister of hers, remember her, her sister's place in Memphis to live…

ROSE. *(She sits.)* You mean Gwen…

BRENDA. That's her, Gwen. Poor pathetic Gwen…Well, we didn't do so well in Memphis either did we Rose…not well at all? What was it, six months before she gave up on us, too…

ROSE. But…

BRENDA. Let me finish, Rose, for Godsake just let me finish…you're the one who started this you know… with this damn phone call of yours…so let me finish …Then after six months and with Mother nowhere in sight, dear old Aunt Gwen hustled you and I off again didn't she…those foster homes this time, remember, "Oh, they will just love having you two young ladies… and you're all so pretty." Well that was a lie, too, Rose, wasn't it?…They didn't love us either…did they? And as for Harriet...well, she got the shaft didn't she...Too old for adoption, isn't that what they said, the adoption agency...Harriet was too old to be adopted?... God knows how she survived.

ROSE. Brenda, please.

BRENDA. Sorry, Rose. You can count me out of this little reunion of yours.

ROSE. *(She stands again.)* But Brenda aren't you interested in even seeing your sisters again, maybe for the last time?

BRENDA. Mail me a picture, how's that?

ROSE. Oh, Brenda, you haven't changed, do you know that, not one bit. Now you sound exactly like the old Brenda.

BRENDA. Just what's that supposed to mean, *I sound like the old Brenda?* Tell me, Rose, what that's supposed to mean?

ROSE. You know exactly what I mean, Brenda. Oh, we were always wrong weren't we, the whole family. You were the only one who knew anything. The rest of us were...were, what did you call us...you know that word you used.

BRENDA. Boring...That was the word I used Rose, boring.

ROSE. Boring, that's it, we were all so boring and conventional weren't we. Uptight right-wingers living in a bubble, you used to say. But not you, oh no, not you, you had to be the free spirit of the family. You always had to be different from us. You always were the smartest one of us girls...winning that scholarship to Berkeley, like you did...we never heard the end of that...you always had to be the person who carried a banner. You always questioned everything didn't you... The radical. Marching in parades for that Caesar Chavez man and his peach pickers...

BRENDA. Grapes. For Godsake Rose, they were grape pickers.

ROSE. Well, whatever they picked. And smoking that pot, you loved unrest, Brenda do you know that, it fit you like a glove.

BRENDA. I loved unrest…I can't believe you just said that…I loved unrest. For Christsake, Rose, we were raised on unrest, don't you understand that? It was fed to us every damn night at that dinner table, a spoonful at a time. And…and you said I loved unrest… Look Rose…

ROSE. Brenda, that's…that's past now…water over the dam…

BRENDA. Rose, must we? Look it was nice of you to call, but…

ROSE. *(stands)* Brenda, wait, don't hang up…think about it…please. Just think about it all right? We are still a family, you know. Even after all of this time, we're still a family.

BRENDA. *(shakes her head slowly, tired of talking with her)* No Rose, I'm tired of even talking about…

ROSE. Brenda, just think about it…please?

BRENDA. *(angrily)* All right…all right, I'll think about it. No promises Rose, you hear me… Do you understand me, no promises I said, but I will think about it. Just think about it, nothing more. Now what's your phone number there?

(All lights go to black.)

Scene Five

(The stage left spot goes on. It is late afternoon. We are again in the living room of **HARRIET COOLEY SMITH** *'s house. She is now awake and sits on the sofa,* **ESTER,** *now wears a very low cut dress and sits next to her. They are talking.)*

ESTER. I just told you…all she said was she was your sister calling you from Muncie, Indiana, some woman named Rose Cooley, that's all I know. Said she was my Aunt for Godsakes…I mean, Mother, how can you forget you have a sister? Things like that aren't that easy to forget you know.

HARRIET. But how did she know I might be her sister?

ESTER. She knew, I told you. She knew a whole lot about you not to be your sister…She said you were adopted! Mother, she said that…adopted. I'm your daughter and even I didn't know that.

*(***ESTER** *looks at her Mother.)*

Why didn't you tell me…why did I have to hear that from some…some stranger…And then there was that cut on you toe, your little one, from when you stepped on that rock…and then the auburn hair…Now how would she know about that if she weren't your sister? Do you think she just picked your name out of the phone book and called…I'm telling you Mother, it was your sister.

HARRIET. It was a piece of glass anyway, Ester, not a rock.

ESTER. See, you do remember. Then its true…all of it…I'll be damned, my Mother has a sister…

HARRIET. Two…

(She looks off in space.)

I have two sisters Ester. Rose Marie and Brenda.

ESTER. Two sisters! That's right. She did say…something about sisters? So why didn't you ever tell me about them or about your being an adopted…

(shakes her head)

ESTER. *(cont.)* My God, then she really is my Aunt…What? Do your sisters all have two heads or something, afraid to let me in on the dark little family secret were you?… Mother, what else haven't you told me…

HARRIET. No, Ester, it's nothing like they didn't have two heads…But…

ESTER. But what?

HARRIET. *(rise)* It was so long ago, Ester…so long since I've even thought about them…since…well you don't understand Ester, you just don't understand.

(turns back to her)

You could never understand.

ESTER. Don't understand what?…Now Mother you just can't say I don't understand and drop it…What is it that you don't think I'll understand?

HARRIET. What it was like back then. What it was like living with…her.

ESTER. Living with who Mother?

HARRIET. With them, Ester, that's who…with my family… my sisters…my Mother…

ESTER. *(Waits as if **HARRIET** is going to continue, but she remains silent.)* And…well…I said and…go on.

HARRIET. Ester you just can't…no one can, not what it was like…not unless you were there.

ESTER. *(with an insistent tone)* Mother…

HARRIET. *(Thinks for a moment and then speaks as if to herself. Looks at her for a beat and then speaks.)* If you must know Ester, my Mother walked out on us, just like my father did…One day we just got up and she left…

*(She turns back to **ESTER**.)*

There are you happy…Now you know.

ESTER. What?…

(She is incredulous.)

She…your…Father…Mother…walked out on you?… You mean just…

HARRIET. Do you know what that felt like Ester…Well, do you? He couldn't take it either…living in that house…that's why he left. But then to just have your Mother walk out on you like that. That's why I never told you…what good would it have done…

(She begins to cry.)

ESTER. *(rises and puts her arms around her)* Mother…Why would she…why would anyone… Mother, you should have told me.

HARRIET. She just had her hair done, you know…All piled on top of her head…then she just kissed us goodbye and walked out …just like she was going to town and do some shopping for the afternoon… She just left us standing there on the front porch of our house with that sister of hers, Gwen…

(ESTER *still holds her mother and looks into her face as she continues.)*

HARRIET. Her sister Gwen.

(She turns and looks at **ESTER.***)*

That's who we ended up living with, Aunt Gwen.

ESTER. Mother, don't…please don't…you don't have to say anything else, really you don't…I'm sorry.

HARRIET. *(continues as if not hearing* **ESTER***'s anger in her voice)* She just walked out on us Ester…it's like it was yesterday, I can still see her…still smell that perfume of hers. I was just seventeen, you know that…I was so young, just seventeen, I never felt so abandoned in my whole life…My own mother just abandoned me.

(looks in **ESTER***'s face)*

Oh, I'm sorry, Ester.

(Long pause then she sits.)

We had to move in with Gwen of course, what else could we do…we were just youngsters for Godsake…

(She slowly shakes her head.)

HARRIET. *(cont.)* How can you do that to youngsters? Gwen lived in Memphis back then…

(Shakes her head.)

That didn't last long though…

(She takes a deep breath and turns to **ESTER** *who is intent on what she has been hearing. She nods her head slowly.)*

After we moved to Memphis, Gwen started getting those migraine headaches of hers, at least that's what she called them, *her migraines.* Said it was our fault of course, the headaches that is. The noise and commotion and all…she'd go to bed for days…all of the shades in the house pulled down, dark and all. We could never play inside of course…oh no, the confusion was too much for her I guess. Then…well then one day when we came home from school there they there waiting for us…

ESTER. *(now incredulous from what she has heard)* Who?…Who was waiting…

HARRIET. *(turns to her)* Why, the people from the adoption agency of course. Two women I think.

ESTER. Adoption agency?…

(a long pause as she processes this)

You can't be serious…

HARRIET. *(stands)* Of course Rose and Brenda were young and pretty back then…they wouldn't have any trouble being placed in foster homes, at least that's what one of the women told Aunt Gwen …but…but as for me…I guess that placing seventeen year-olds aren't as easy…

ESTER. What do you mean Mother…not as easy…

HARRIET. *(now angry)* Why Ester, that means I was on my own…abandoned again…

(softly cries)

I was too old to be in a foster home…that's what that means. Who wants a seventeen year-old anyway?

ESTER. *(throws her arms around her neck)* Oh, my God…
Mother…I'm sorry,

HARRIET. *(She holds* ESTER.*)* I never needed anyone more
in my life then I did back there in Memphis…now
that's the truth, Ester. I swear to God it is. I had such
a need for someone to just take me in their arms and
hold me, hold me like you're holding me now…Just
someone to tell me that everything was all right. Just to
know that I counted for something…

*(A long pause as she composes herself. She dries her eyes
with the back of her hand and turns to* ESTER.*)*

Now Ester, everything is all right.

(She pats ESTER *on the back.)*

It's past now…everything is fine I tell you. And child,
that's why I never told you any of this…It was just too
painful…Why that was so long ago…It's just that…
well, now to hear that one of my sisters has found me…
and after all this time, it just all comes back, sudden
like …just now…the memories and all… I just need a
little time to think about this, I really do…that's all…

ESTER. Then you're all right…really?

HARRIET. *(She sits.)* Yes, Ester, I'm fine…really.

ESTER. *(a brief pause)* Are you going to call her back?

HARRIET. Now Ester, you know that your mother doesn't
deal with crisis very well.

*(She reaches for her Bible, which sits on the small table
next to the sofa.)*

I just need to work my way through the peaks and val-
leys of my indecision…

ESTER. Mother, but what about your sister in Muncie…you
are going to call her?

HARRIET. I need to…I just need some support before I call
her, Ester…Oh how I wish your father was still alive,
he'd tell me what to do, he always knew what to do…
No, no Ester, I can't call her back, not until I call

Pastor Wilby. I require some spiritual guidance…you know that. This is a big decision for me it might affect my whole life…Once I talk to him…

ESTER. But Mother…

HARRIET. *(She turns to* **ESTER.***)* No, Ester, Pastor Wilby is the one I need now…He'll know what to do.

ESTER. But Mother, I can help you…if you like?

HARRIET. *(She turns to* **ESTER** *and takes her in her arms and give her a hug. Then she gently moves her away and smiles still holding here at arms length.)* I know you can dear, but I have to call Pastor Wilby. This might be a sign…you know from…

(She points up.)

ESTER. A sign…Mother, it's just a phone call…a simple little phone call from your sister, that's all. Not some…

(She groups for the right word and then simply points towards the ceiling.)

Don't you understand…just a simple phone call.

HARRIET. But its been forty-years, Ester…forty-years…What do I say?

ESTER. Mother it's your sister just say…

(a long beat)

Hello.

HARRIET. But it could be a sign, Ester, truly it could be… Pastor Wilby said I was due one you know. Anytime now he said and this might be it. Just think this might be the big one. My own personal epiphany just dropped into my lap…plop…just like that…

ESTER. *(ignores her comment)* Now look Mother. It's me, Ester talking.

*(***HARRIET** *nods.)*

Say someday I might decide to get married, maybe want children…Well I'd want to know just where my roots had been planted and who planted them…what kind of soil I came from…gene pools, things that get passed down to you in families that you don't even know about…I don't want to find out someday that this sister of yours, my dear old Aunt Rose, has lost a boob or some other body part along the line because of some crummy little gene that she might have gotten from your side of the family.

(She holds out a handful of hair.)

I mean look…Who knows what's swimming around in there, what to expect from your family?…So you see, that is why you have got to call her…for my sake, because I want to know that some day one of those genes isn't going to jump up an bite me on my butt. So just call her…please.

HARRIET. But Ester…you don't know my sisters, if you did… Well, one of them, Brenda, was a marcher…you know, like one of those radicals you see on TV…picketing at conventions… protesting…waving around signs like… well, like, "Show them you're a woman, Burn your Bra!"…arms locked together…all screaming…

ESTER. *(holds her hands up for silence)* Mother…I said are you going to call her?…Yes or no?

HARRIET. *(She stops speaking, knowing her cause is lost. She looks at* **ESTER** *and slowly nods.)* Yes…yes, Ester, I'll call her.

(All lights go to black.)

Scene Six

*(Centerstage light comes on. **BRENDA** still sits in the
wing chair thinking as her husband **JEFFREY** enters the
room. He is a black gentleman who wears jeans and a
college T-shirt. He carries two glasses of wine. He offers
one to her.)*

JEFFREY. I thought you might still be on the phone so I
brought you some fortification...Say, who was that
anyway, you were flapping for quite a while.

BRENDA. My sister...Can you believe it and after all these
years I get a call from my sister...

(She takes the glass of wine.)

Thanks, my sweet.

JEFFREY. Your what? Your sister, I didn't know you had a
sister.

BRENDA. I don't Jeffrey, I have two of them. Rose Marie
and Harriet Jean...Count them...two. And now after
all this time one of them calls me.

JEFFREY. Whoa...now this is getting heavy. Two sisters.

BRENDA. God, it's been forty-years since I've even thought
about them, even remembered having sisters, it
seemed like I was always an only child...

(She looks at him.)

I told you about them Jeffrey, don't you remember,
back at Berkeley, you probably had just forgotten...I
know I'd told you...And now...today of all days one of
them calls me.

(She takes a sip of her wine.)

JEFFREY. Well what did she want, this sister of yours, you
know the one I should have remembered, the one you
told me about, what was it, forty-years ago?

BRENDA. She wants to get together, to get the *girls* together
for one last meet and greet before the drums of doom
beat our final retreat I suppose.

JEFFREY. What?…Brenda just what in the hell are you talking about. Drums of doom…

BRENDA. Oh, Jeffrey…I just told you, my sister Rose just called and wants the three Cooley girls to get together, a reunion and after all this time, you know press the flesh, hugs and kisses, tell a few lies, show each other pictures of the kids and dogs…and the rose covered cottages we call home I suppose and then just turn around and go home as if it had never happened…

(She looks at him.)

How in the hell do I know what she wants?

JEFFREY. Easy girl, easy…You're going to go aren't you?

BRENDA. *(looks up at him)* Oh, sure, in a pig's eye I am going ….You can't be serious Jeffrey. It's been years since… well, too many years to just pick-up and start again… go to some reunion…recapture whatever it was…I told you what life was like in that house, I hated it! What's to recapture. What do we have in common? No one had a social conscience back then but me…white bread, Mary Poppins, Republicans, that was them. No…It's been too long now to go back and trace my roots thank you…Hell, I planted new ones of my own when I met you.

JEFFREY. I know all about that Brenda, but they still are your sisters, they'll always be your sisters, I mean you can't hide from that. Hell, you white folk sure squander your heritage, I swear to God you do. Christ, Brenda you'd be the first one to run off into that woods out there and hug a damn tree, but when the time comes to hug a sister, sorry two sisters…You all should just get down on yours knees and thank the Almighty that you have roots to trace. Look at me, if I go back more than three generations I run right into a stonewall. Splat. That's it. Zip. Nothing. Past that, *I ain't got no history ma'am.*

BRENDA. Jeffrey, please.

(She rises and stands to the right of the chair and continues.)

BRENDA. *(cont.)* I'm not a student in your classroom, I don't need to hear all of this...especially not in dialect.

JEFFREY. Oh, yes you do, they're your sisters for Godsake. That's what you have in common. They're your sisters. Aren't you curious...Hey, just stifle that angry little Jane Fonda that lives inside you for a while and go. Babe, no Republican can be that bad, honey, no matter who they are or what they did...Did you tell her you would come?

BRENDA. No.

JEFFREY. No?

BRENDA. No...I...well, I told her I had to think about it.

JEFFREY. You told her you'd think about it! ...That was it... You told her you'd *think about it.* Now just what in the hell does that mean...I am going to think about it? That is a non-answer Brenda, and you know it. Either you are going or you're not. Which is it?

BRENDA. I don't know what I want to do for God's sake, that's what it means.

(She turns and sits again in the chair.)

Oh, Jeffrey help me.

JEFFREY. Sorry...this is you family, Brenda, and you are going to have to be the one that make this call.

BRENDA. But can't you see...I can't.

JEFFREY. No, Brenda I can only see that you don't want to...look Brenda you can't always be the only one who is right in this life and everyone one else be wrong.

BRENDA. *(looks at him for several beats)* Who said anything about my being right?

JEFFREY. Oh, come on Brenda. In your eyes your family was never right, just you. You want the truth honey....Well, do you...

(pause)

You're afraid...

BRENDA. *(sits up)* Afraid...me. Afraid of what?

JEFFREY. *(Moves to her. He speaks quietly.)* Afraid of yourself, that's who you're afraid of...you. Didn't you just say you don't even remember having sisters, that you always felt like an only child...

(She nods her head,)

See...you're afraid of how to accept them after all this time...afraid they won't accept you....Isn't that it?

BRENDA. That's not it and you know it...not it at all... afraid.

JEFFREY. Brenda, then what? If you're not afraid then what is it? Just tell me and then I'll just stop asking.

(Sits staring off for several beats taking in what he has just said. Then she slowly looks up to him and begins to nod her head in agreement.)

BRENDA. *(quietly)* I guess I am afraid...afraid of myself... Oh, Jeffrey, hell what am I supposed to do?...I don't want to call her back, I really don't...I'm afraid of what it might lead too, bring back all...remind me of...

(pause)

But then again I do want to call...

(She looks at him.)

Help me, for Godsake?

JEFFREY. You call her...you hear me, just pick up the phone Brenda and call her. It'll be fine.

BRENDA. But Jeffrey...

JEFFREY. *(He puts his hand to her mouth.)* No buts please, just call her...You'll be all right...if marching in Selma didn't scare you...calling your sister should be a piece of cake...Look, I have my last class in June...June the third. Hell, I'll even drive you out to Kennedy airport...

(He looks at her as if asking where does she live.)

BRENDA. But, Jeffrey...

(JEFFREY points to the phone)

(**BRENDA** *reaches for the phone, then looks at* **JEFFREY** *and pulls him towards her and gives him another kiss.*)

(*All lights go to black.*)

Scene Seven

(Lights at stage left come up revealing **HARRIET** *sitting on the sofa now dressed in a muumuu. Next to her on the table sits her Bible. She dials the phone. As the phone begins to ring the stage right lights come up. It is* **ROSE***'s house again. After several rings* **ROSE** *enters stage right picks up the phone. The action begins.)*

ROSE. Hello?

HARRIET. *(There is a long pause.)*

ROSE. Hello?

HARRIET. Rose?

ROSE. Yes, this is Rose…who is this?

HARRIET. It's me, your sister. Harriet, your sister in Pula Springs…

ROSE. *(surprise in her voice)* Did you say, Harriet…Really is this you?

HARRIET. Yes, Rose. I said it was Harriet. Ester said that you had called…Now, why did you call and after all of this time?

ROSE. Oh, Harriet, I can't believe it's you. I mean that you would call back, that we, that you and I are actually talking to each other and after all of these years. I think I am going to cry.

HARRIET. Stop it Rose, this call is costing me and I don't intend to pay out good money just to hear you cry, so no tears…Now why did you call after all this…

ROSE. Oh, Harriet, I am just wonderful now, now that you've called, really I am. And you…how are you? And you have a daughter.

HARRIET. Rose, I said, I need to know why you called?

ROSE. I just called to see how you were, where you were, what you were doing…find you girls again, truly I did…oh, I nearly forgot…guess what? I've talked with Brenda, today…I did. She lives in New York State, can you believe it…New York State.

HARRIET. *(She stands.)* Brenda…Did you say Brenda…so you found her too did you…Oh good heavens, why did you go and do a thing like that…that radical…is she still out there waving that flag of hers?

ROSE. Now Harriet what a thing to say and after all this time. Why you never used to say a word against any one…That's why we all looked up to you…You were so…well so…

HARRIET. Oh, stop it, Rose. Do you hear me, just stop it…I never said anything against anyone…That's because I never had any reason to, that is not until…

ROSE. Not until what, Harriet?

HARRIET. For Godsake you know…since we were thrown out…packed off to Memphis…abandoned like we were…that's what changed me….

(She sits.)

What probably changed all of us.

ROSE. Now Harriet, it was not that bad…

HARRIET. Not that bad! I can't believe…and from you of all people. That it was not that bad?…Well Rose, it was, for me it was that bad. Do you hear me?

ROSE. I only meant…

HARRIET. I don't care what you meant. I only know that you…well that you and Brenda will never know what it was like for me. What I had to live through.

ROSE. Now, Harriet…

HARRIET. Well, you don't… Having that rug pulled out from under me like that…no place to go…no one to…being alone like I was… I needed things Rose, do you know that, I needed things…

ROSE. Things…

HARRIET. Someone to hold onto, Rose…something to believe in. That's when I found him…

ROSE. Him?

HARRIET. God, Rose…The one person who would never give up on me never be far from me. That's who I found…Now, why did you call?

ROSE. I told you, I had to find you and Brenda. It's been too long for all of us not to have made some effort to find one another…The idea just came to me two months ago…really it did. I know this sounds crazy, but it happened at the kitchen sink. I was just standing there in the kitchen at the sink doing the dishes when it just popped into my mind…find Harriet, find Brenda…just like that…just that suddenly it came to me…like some tiny voice was talking to me, telling me to find you both. I could even see your faces. Now doesn't that sound silly, me seeing your faces?

HARRIET. *(reacts to her words and stands)* You say it just came to you, in the kitchen, at the sink…that you could see our faces…

ROSE. Truly it did…just like that…now doesn't that sound ridiculous.

HARRIET. *(gasps)* No, no not at all…My God it must be a sign, Rose…a sign from up there…

(She points over her head.)

Oh Rose, you have had an epiphany…a real, bonafide epiphany…You had your very own epiphany.

ROSE. Nonsense, Harriet. It…it was nothing like that at all.

HARRIET. No, Rose, I'm sure of it…Pastor Wilby said mine was coming you know, at any time, my very own epiphany, but mine must have gotten short circuited somehow and came to you by mistake…well, it would now wouldn't it, you are my sister after all, it can happen. I guess things like that run in families, epiphanies that is…

ROSE. Harriet, really what a thing to say…an epiphany runs in families…

HARRIET. *(We can see she has just had an idea.)* I nearly forgot…

(Her voice changes as again)

Speaking of things running in families Rose, I have to ask you a very personal question? Ester asked me…

ROSE. Ester…A personal question you say…

HARRIET. Something she read in a magazine…

ROSE. I see…well, what is it…What does she want to know?

HARRIET. Rose, have you ever lost any body parts…Arms, things like that?

ROSE. What on earth are you talking about?

HARRIET. Just forget I even asked, it's not important, I told her it was a silly question. Now, Rose about your call. What did you want?

ROSE. *(stands)* I want you and Brenda and I to meet, to meet again. Here in Muncie, Indiana, at my house for a long weekend…a reunion of sorts. Just we three, the Cooley girls together again after all this time, you will come won't you…please?

HARRIET. A reunion…in Muncie, Indian…

(She becomes nervous.)

Oh Rose, I…well, I don't know about that…I mean… well there is so much to consider…Who would stay with Ester and then there's my church work. I am very dedicated to my Church and then…well, then there is Pastor Wilby…well, I would have to talk to him about this…about making a trip all that way to…Well, all the way to Indiana. I mean you just can't throw a change of clothes into a bag and pick up and go you know… It's just not that easy.

ROSE. Harriet…Something's wrong isn't it? I can tell it.

HARRIET. Wrong…What do you mean, something is wrong?

(becomes very uncomfortable and looks about hoping to find the right words)

It's just that I need some time to plan for a trip like this that's all…I mean I get this call from you…and after all these years…and I'm just expected to drop everything…I just need some time to sort things out, you know that's all…

ROSE. No…no, Harriet. Now what in the world is the problem?

HARRIET. *(sits)* Rose, please…Don't you know how hard this is for me…to finally hear from one of you and after all this time? If I say yes Rose…well…well, then I'll have to open up that box I always kept closed inside of me…free those memories of us when were children, living in that house…You know what we went through…bring out everything…all that hurt I've tried to forget…It's too painful…don't you understand that…Just give me some time Rose, that's all I need some time…

ROSE. Then are you are coming or not?…Well, Harriet, are you?

(a long pause)

HARRIET. *(reluctantly)* All right Rose. All right…Yes…yes, I'm coming.

(All lights go to black.)

Scene Eight

*(Lights at centerstage come up as we again see **BRENDA**. She is seated and dials the phone next to her. Beside her stands **JEFFREY**. As it begins to ring lights come up at stage right, **ROSE**'s home. After several rings **ROSE** enters stage right and answers. Action begins.)*

ROSE. Yes.

BRENDA. Rose…it's me…Brenda, I said I would call you back.

ROSE. Yes, Brenda…I know you did. No promises you said, you'd think about it you said…Then this call…does it mean you're coming…Just tell me that you're coming?

BRENDA. *(Looks up at **JEFFREY** who stands next to her, he holds her hand.)* Yes, Rose. I am coming.

ROSE. Oh, Brenda, I…well, I'm so…I can't believe it you're really coming.

BRENDA. Yes, Rose, I'm really coming.

ROSE. You are…you really are…

BRENDA. Yes, Rose, I cross my heart.

(She crosses her heart.)

I'm really coming.

ROSE. Oh, Brenda…

*(**ROSE** looks off for a minute.)*

You used to do that all the time, did you know that… whenever you had made up your mind to do something really important in your life…you always crossed your heart.

BRENDA. *(slowly shakes her head in amazement)* Yes, Rose, I guess I did do that, so you still remember. I'm afraid that you remembered more that I have. Well, goodbye Rose.

ROSE. Yes, goodbye Brenda, and thank you. I'll let you and Harriet know the dates and all, how would that be?

(Lights go to black.)

End Act One

ACT TWO

Scene One

*(It is several months later. The scene is **ROSE**'s apartment in Muncie, Indiana. To stage right sits **ROSE**'s phone table, center stage sits the sofa and side table, to stage left sits the wing chair, floor lamp and table. A coffee table sits in front of the sofa, a vase of fresh flowers sits atop it. The action begins, as **ROSE** enters from stage right. She is dressed in a modest dress, her hair worn in a conservative 'Republican' hairstyle. Around her neck she wears a single strand of pearls, her glasses hang over it attached to a gold metal chain. She stops and surveys the scene before her, then walks to the coffee table and rearranges the vase of flowers. She steps backs as she inspects the room. Suddenly she remembers something and hastily leaves the room only to return several moments later holding a framed picture, which she dusts with her hand before putting this too on the coffee table next to the flowers. Now she nods her approval, the scene is set. We hear a knock at the door as the action begins.)*

ROSE. I'll be right there…just a minute.

(She presses the front of her dress with her hands, takes a breath and exits stage left to the front door. We hear voices.)

HARRIET. Rose?…It's me, Harriet…my heavens is that you?…It really is you isn't it and after all these years.

ROSE. Oh, Harriet, yes…yes it's me…come in, please come in. You look wonderful, just wonderful. Here let me take your bag…

HARRIET. Nonsense Rose, I may be your older sister, but I am still capable of carrying my own bag.

*(They both enter the room. **HARRIET**'s auburn hair is worn short, she is dressed in a causal jacket worn over a lightweight sweater and skirt. We can now see the family resemblance. At her neck is a large cross on a chain. She carries a small suitcase. Once in the room she puts the suitcase down and takes a step back)*

HARRIET. *(cont.)* Now…don't move…Just stand there for a minute so I can really look at you.

*(She inspects **ROSE** closely as if looking for lost body parts.)*

Now turn around.

*(**ROSE** does.)*

Well goodness you seem to be all there don't you, now give me a kiss.

*(**ROSE** does.)*

It's wonderful seeing you again…and after all this time. Oh, Rose, you won't believe what a trip I've had getting here…I mean it…twenty-nine hours and thirty-four minutes on that bus, can you believe it twenty-nine hours…and thirty-four minutes…but…well, I'm here.

ROSE. Yes, here you are at last.

HARRIET. Just thank the Lord for Pastor Wilby.

ROSE. Pastor Wilby. Who's that?

HARRIET. Pastor Wilby, my pastor, back in Pula Springs, at the Mount Zion Church of the First Creation of course. I mean without his help I could never have done this…never. He drove me to the bus station, bless his heart…all the way to Reno, that dear man.

*(looks at **ROSE**)*

And such a Saint, Rose, a true Saint…He's what you might call my spiritual advisor…my guide in this life so to speak…He is always there for me…always. Of course he insisted on praying over me at the bus station.

(She looks up and closes her eyes one hand held high over her head.)

HARRIET. *(cont.)* Lord watch over your servant Harriet here on her pilgrimage by Greyhound to Muncie Indiana to visit her long lost sister Rose…

(pause)

And guide her in her every footstep.

(looks at **ROSE***)*

Such a religious human being.

ROSE. *(a bit befuddled)* Yes…yes he must be…

(She takes her hands.)

Oh, Harriet, I can't believe it's you, really I can't. My very own sister standing right here in my living room in Muncie, Indiana and after all this…well, I just can't believe it. Now here just let me get your bag.

*(***ROSE*** picks up the bag.)*

I have the guest room all set up for you. It's over here… just follow me and I'll show you.

(They both turn and walk stage right and exit we can still hear their voices.)

HARRIET. Oh, Rose, what a real cute place you have here.

ROSE. And that is the bathroom and over here is your room, well, the room you and Brenda will be sharing.

HARRIET. You mean I have to sleep in the same room with that…that storm trooper?

ROSE. Now Harriet Jean, don't talk like that. It's only for a weekend and I am sure being such a religious person, as you are, you can surely suffer through just one weekend with your *sister.*

(They return.)

Besides it's the only spare room I have.

HARRIET. *(smiles)* I guess you're right, Rose…we all have our crosses to bear in this life, I suspect Brenda will just have to be mine. It's fine, really it is.

(almost to herself)

As Pastor Wilby has often said, this too shall pass.

ROSE. (**ROSE** *does not hear her comment.*) What?

HARRIET. I said…here at last…You know the bus trip.

ROSE. Well, of course, you are and after that long bus trip you must be tired. And I am just standing here talking on and on, come sit here.

(*She points to the wing chair.*)

How silly of me. May I get you anything to drink?

(**ROSE** *sits and smiles*)

HARRIET. Something to drink? Well, of course I am parched heavens knows, that bus trip and all…a drink would be wonderful…just a small glass of…

ROSE. (*She cuts* **HARRIET** *'s line.*) Water, a soft drink or something stronger?

(**ROSE** *smiles.*)

HARRIET. That sounds perfect Rose, yes, just perfect… Something stronger.

ROSE. Then you just sit there and I'll be right back.

(*She turns towards the kitchen, stage right and moves*).

I just made some lemonade it should be cold by now.

(*She exits.*)

HARRIET. Did you say…

(*flatly*)

Lemonade?

ROSE. (*from off stage*) Yes, is that all right?

HARRIET. That sounds wonderful Rose. Just what I was hoping for after a sixteen-hour bus trip…a glass of lukewarm…*lemonade.*

(*We hear another knock at the door.* **HARRIET** *turns and looks as* **ROSE** *calls from the kitchen.*)

Scene Two

ROSE. Oh, Harriet could you see who that is? It might be Brenda.

HARRIET. Must I…

ROSE. *(from kitchen)* Now, now…remember that cross you have to bear…

HARRIET. *(Looks to the kitchen then stands. Then hesitates. Reluctantly she goes to the door as again we hear voices.)* Why, look who's here…this must be Brenda?

BRENDA. Why, don't tell me, let me guess…this must be… is it Harriet Jean?

HARRIET. Well come in, Rose is in the kitchen.

(The two sisters enter silently. **BRENDA** *is dressed in jeans, sandals and wears a T-shirt with the words* "LEAVE IRAQ NOW" *boldly printed across it. Her hair is still wildly going in all directions a hair band at her forehead. She carries a canvas duffle bag. The two stand facing each other, neither one speaks. After several beats:)*

It's been some time.

BRENDA. *(without expression)* Yes…it has been some time.

HARRIET. *(without expression)* You…you look well.

BRENDA. *(without expression)* So do you.

HARRIET. I can see you haven't changed much…still picketing.

(She nods.)

The shirt…

BRENDA. *(a bite to her voice)* No I haven't changed, Harriet, and by the looks of it neither have you.

HARRIET. *(with some forcefulness now)* I suppose we never do change do we, Brenda?

BRENDA. *(She takes a step closer to* **HARRIET** *so that they are standing almost nose to nose.)* Look here, Harriet, I know you never thought much of me when we were growing up, but I haven't come all this way to allow you to play that older sister bit again, especially after all of this time. Now, if we are going to be spending this *brief* weekend together as *sisters* let's at least be civil to one another, ok…Now don't push it.

HARRIET. I don't know what you're talking about.

BRENDA. Oh, yes you do, that sound in your voice, that holier then thou attitude of yours. I was wondering if you'd changed…but I can see you haven't.

HARRIET. You even sound like her…

BRENDA. Just who might that be Harriet, or am I to guess?

HARRIET. Mother of course, you always were her favorite.

BRENDA. Look here…

ROSE. *(enters the room with* **HARRIET**'*s glass of lemonade and gives it to her)* Brenda…Brenda …Brenda Cooley is that you…well, don't you tell me that this is you and after all these years.

(She moves to her and hands the glass off to **HARRIET** *and then takes* **BRENDA** *in her arms and hugs her.)*

Brenda, you…you look…Oh, I am going to cry, I just know it. I am going to just burst out in tears right here in front of you both.

(She holds **BRENDA** *about the waist and then reaches out for* **HARRIET**. *Now the three of them stand in* **ROSE**'*s embrace.* **BRENDA** *and* **HARRIET** *look away from each other.)*

Just look, the Cooley girls are together again…just think of it and after all of this time, one big happy family again.

BRENDA. *(flatly)* Yes…just think of it.

ROSE. *(looking at* **HARRIET***)* Isn't this wonderful, Harriet, just the three of us together again, it's like old times, isn't it?

HARRIET. *(no emotion)* That's us…one big happy family.

ROSE. *(noticing that she still holds her duffle bag)* Oh my, Brenda, here let me take that for you and I'll show you your room.

BRENDA. That's all right Rose, I have it…You just point the way.

ROSE. *(She turns and leads* **BRENDA** *off stage to 'the bedroom.')* Your room is right in here. You and Harriet are going to be sharing the guest room…that's all right isn't it, I mean you don't mind do you?

*(***ROSE** *exits.)*

BRENDA. No…no, Rose, that will be fine…just fine. If she snores…

(turns back to **HARRIET***)*

I guess I'll just have to *smother* her with a pillow in her sleep.

*(***HARRIET** *sits in the wing chair and looks at the glass of lemonade in her hand as if it is poison, then shudders before placing it on the table next to the wing chair.)*

ROSE. *(enters the room with* **BRENDA***)* I hope you like the room, Brenda?

BRENDA. It's fine, Rose.

ROSE. Now you just sit down…there on the sofa

(She indicates with her hand.)

That's it right there…Would you like something to drink…Water, a soft drink or perhaps something stronger…I have just made some…

BRENDA. *(cuts her line)* Do you have any scotch in the house, Rose?

(She looks towards **HARRIET***.)*

I think I need a drink.

*(***HARRIET** *sits bolt upright in her chair.)*

ROSE. Scotch, you say. Oh, I'm sure I have a bottle of it somewhere in the kitchen…just let me look.

HARRIET. Scotch…I did hear you say scotch, didn't I?

ROSE. Yes, Harriet, I think I have a bottle in the kitchen.

HARRIET. If it's not too much trouble Rose…well, do you think I might have just a…well just a little bitty tiny glass of scotch.

(indicates with her fingers)

Just two fingers on the rocks no water…the bus trip you know…

ROSE. *(looks towards the glass of lemonade sitting next to her on the table)* Why of course, no trouble at all. I'll be right back.

(BRENDA goes to the sofa and sits. She looks straight ahead as does HARRIET. They each try and glance at the other but quickly turn away thinking the other is doing the same. Neither say a word. Both just look about the room ignoring one another. After several moments ROSE returns with two very small glasses of scotch. She gives one to BRENDA and the other to HARRIET.)

ROSE. Now, are we having fun yet girls…I hope you two are getting re-acquainted?

(Both BRENDA and HARRIET just stare at ROSE.)

BRENDA. Aren't you going to have anything Rose?

ROSE. Well…maybe because this is such a special occasion.

(She leans over and picks up the glass of lemonade from the table next to HARRIET and holds it up.)

I'll just have this glass of lemonade.

(Then she returns to the sofa and sits next BRENDA. The room falls silent for a moment as no one speaks. Then ROSE looks around and as almost an after thought raises her glass.)

Well, *girls*, cheers.

HARRIET. *(flatly)* Cheers.

(Without enthusiasm, BRENDA merely lifts her glass and silently joins in. They all drink. HARRIET downs hers in one gulp as she turns and glares at BRENDA. Once again the room falls silent for several beats. Then as if on cue they all begin to talk, their words over lapping.)

ROSE. My Harriet you must have been…

BRENDA. Rose how long have you lived in….

HARRIET. Might I have another, the bus trip…

(They all look to one another. Silence again. Then they speak again.)

BRENDA. *(looks at* **HARRIET,** *an edge to her voice)* I was just going to ask Rose, how long she has lived here in Muncie?

ROSE. Oh, twenty-years, yes twenty-years next September.

HARRIET. *(to* **BRENDA** *firmly)* Well, I was just going to ask Rose if I might have just one more tiny one, that's all.

(She holds up her glass to **ROSE.** *)*

You know the…

BRENDA. *(sarcastically)* The bus trip, wasn't that it Harriet, the bus trip.

ROSE. *(She turns to* **HARRIETT.** *)* There is more in the kitchen Harriet, please help yourself.

HARRIET. Yes, you're right as usual, Brenda…the bus trip.

(She rises and crosses to the kitchen.)

ROSE. *(interjects to ease the tension)* And how long have you lived New York State Brenda, it seems like such a pretty state… Is it…pretty that is?

BRENDA. Since we graduated from Berkeley.

*(***HARRIET*** enters holding her new drink.)*

ROSE. *(to* **BRENDA***)* You…you said we. Does that mean that you're…

BRENDA. Yes. I'm married, Rose. That happened right after I graduated from Berkeley, too. He and I were in the same political science class. He was an Assistant Professor.

ROSE. Of course you're married, how silly of me…I nearly forgot, Brenda Chatsworth, well you would have to be married then wouldn't you.

(She laughs softly.)

An Assistant Professor you said…my how nice…Do you have any children?

BRENDA. No, it's just the two of us, just Jeffrey and me.

ROSE. Jeffrey, my what a nice name…

(beat)

So then we've all married.

(She looks at her two sisters.)

What do you think of that…I was married once you know. Oh, I know that doesn't sound possible does it, little Rose Cooley getting married, but I was, you know, his name was Henry…Oh, we didn't have any children either…a tipped uterus.

HARRIET. A tipped uterus?…Oh, Rose, that's awful.

(She thinks a moment.)

Is that inherited…does it run in families. Does that have anything to do with genes?

ROSE. No, I don't think so Harriet.

BRENDA. *(ignores HARRIET's comment)* Rose, what does your Henry do?

ROSE. *(looks down for a moment)* Well before he passed on four years ago he was a shipping clerk, for Sears and Roebuck, you know the people with the catalog…He worked right here in Muncie. Oh, he loved his job.

(HARRIET takes a drink as they continue to talk.)

BRENDA. I'm sorry to hear about your Henry, Rose…

HARRIET. *(She looks up and joins in.)* Well, it comes to all of us you know…When our time comes to enter that long dark tunnel for our trip to the other side, how can we refuse…Just like with my Bernard, here one minute gone the next…but I suppose he was needed up there.

(She points to the ceiling.)

On some special assignment I'm sure.

ROSE. Special assignment? Oh, Harriet, what did he do, your Bernard? That is before…

(Now she points up.)

You know.

HARRIET. *(She nods.)* Bowling alleys.

ROSE. Bowling alleys?

HARRIET. Yes, Rose, bowling alleys, Lanes Galore in Pula Springs, he was half owner...We used to bowl every Wednesday and Saturday night.

BRENDA. *(finishes her drink in a gulp)* Bowling alleys for Godsake.

ROSE. *(looks at her)* Brenda would you like another drink... your glass seems to be empty. It's in the kitchen so please help yourself, you too Harriet. Why after all we are family...This is your home now too I suppose.

BRENDA. If you don't mind Rose...I think I'm going to need it.

*(She looks at **HARRIET** then stands and starts towards the kitchen.)*

HARRIET. Well...just look at this will you.

(She holds up her empty glass.)

My glass seems to be empty too...I think I'll join Brenda in the kitchen and fix another if I may.

(She to stands and starts towards the kitchen.)

ROSE. *(smiles)* You two go right ahead...help yourselves.

(to herself)

My they seem happy...

HARRIET. *(She sticks her head from the kitchen. In her hand she holds an opened bottle of vodka.)* Rose, did you know you had this?

*(**ROSE** looks up.)*

Now you just come right out here. There's nothing like a good shot or two of vodka in a glass of lemonade.

ROSE. But...

HARRIET. *(**HARRIET** takes **ROSE** and pulls her towards the kitchen.)* None of that, come on Rose, this is a party after all...what did you say.

(She turns back to the kitchen.)

HARRIET. *(cont.)* Brenda, what did Rose say this was going to be…You know, our getting together like this…What did she call it?

BRENDA. You mean a reunion Harriett…Is that the word you're trying to think of…Reunion?

HARRIET. That's it. A reunion, a reunion party.

ROSE. Well…just a bit perhaps. I guess you're right…this really is a party, isn't it?

(She stands and goes to the kitchen. After a pause)

Not so much Harriet…

(In a moment we hear laughter coming from the kitchen. Then **BRENDA, HARRIET** *and* **ROSE** *re-enter, each now has a drink. They raise their glasses to one another.)*

Scene Three

ROSE. *(taking a sip of her drink)* Harriet this is so good, I can't taste anything though except the lemonade.

BRENDA. You will Rose, you will.

HARRIET. Rose do you remember that time you brought home that cat you found, you know the one with the bobbed tail, that silly looking cat you wanted to keep.

(She sits.)

You used to call him…Shorty, I think. Do you remember that?

BRENDA. Bobbie. She called him Bobbie, Harriet, not Shorty.

(She sits.)

HARRIET. *(looks at* **BRENDA***)* Why what a name for a cat… Bobbie?…No, I think she called it Shorty.

(She tries to recall.)

Are you sure it was, Bobbie?

BRENDA. Yes, Harriet. I am sure. It was Bobbie…his bobbed tail…understand…Bobbed…Bobbie.

ROSE. *(sits)* You're right Brenda, it was Bobbie. And that silly stump of a tail of his…the poor creature.

BRENDA. *(begins to laugh)* No, no Rose, the funny part was when Bobbie had six kittens.

HARRIET. Yes, you're right even I remember that…My word of course I do, she had them under my bed…how could I forget?

(They all laugh.)

ROSE. Oh, that's a fact, Bobby turned out to be Miss Bobbie didn't she?

(thinks for a moment)

But then who was the boy who had a crush on Harriet here? Don't you remember him? He lived over on the next block, wasn't his name Bobby…I think he had the eye problem or something like that.

BRENDA. You're right, the boy with the crossed eyes.

HARRIET. *(takes a sip of her drink)* Now just a minute here, who was this…just who are you taking about now. Are you saying I would go out with a boy with crossed eyes? I never dated any boy with crossed eyes…

ROSE. Yes, you did Harriet. He was that usher down at the Rialto Theater. The one you had such a crush on. Why you couldn't stay away from him…you had to go to the movies ever Saturday afternoon just so you could see him, don't you remember? His name was, Dwayne, wasn't that it…Dwayne Markham.

(takes another drink)

BRENDA. Right again, that's the one…Dwayne Markham.

HARRIET. He didn't have crossed eyes…both of you are wrong. They just drooped, that's all…just drooped. He was tired… Heavens, you both know he worked in that dark theater for ten hours a day…I mean anyone's eyes would droop after being on their feet in a dark place like that for ten hours…And while we are subject of boys…Don't forget Randy 'The Octopus'…you know that boy Brenda, I'm sure, the boy who used to date you.

*(She looks at **BRENDA**.)*

Randy the octopus, the boy with eight arms, I'll never forget him.

BRENDA. Oh, Harriet. He was no 'octopus.'

HARRIET. Oh, yes he was. Ask Rose here, she used to spy on you two whenever he brought you home after a date… the two of you just standing there in the hall…being pawed like that.

*(looks to **ROSE**)*

Now didn't you, Rose?

*(She looks at **BRENDA**.)*

You used to tell me all about it.

ROSE. Harriet you didn't have to tell her that!

HARRIET. My God Rose, why not, it was forty-years ago.

BRENDA. *(takes a sip of her drink and looks off for a moment)* Randy Lawton.

(She begins to slowly shake her head.)

My, God you're right. I'd forgotten him…Randy Lawton. Come to think of it he was an octopus.

ROSE. *(shocked)* Oh! Brenda…

(Now they all laugh.)

ROSE. *(leans forward)* Now, girls. I'll bet neither of you remember Raymond, Raymond Tuttle? Do you?

BRENDA. Raymond?

HARRIET. *(thinks then holds her hand up)* I do, I do. He was that boy who lived right across the street from us wasn't he? The one with those crooked teeth…that boy who proposed to you when you were both in the fourth grade, wasn't that him?

ROSE. *(She nods.)* That was him…oh he had such a crush on me back then. We'd eat lunch together every day in the school cafeteria…He used to give me half of his peanut butter sandwich…did you know that…well he did…You know, to this day I still dislike peanut butter.

(They laugh.)

BRENDA. I remember him now. Tall, red hair and glasses? Didn't he come to the Halloween party we had one year in the basement…the boy who was dressed as a scarecrow…wasn't that him?

ROSE. No that was Harry Wright…he was the scarecrow. Raymond was dressed as Superman, at least I think he was Superman.

HARRIET. You're right Rose, he was.

(She begins to laugh.)

Remember he almost drowned when that Kendall boy held his head under water for so long when we were bobbing for apples…scared him so much I think he wet himself didn't he?

BRENDA. Said he was only trying to help him get a better grip on the apple…

ROSE. No, he didn't wet himself. It was just some water from the apple dunking, when he tried to get away from that Kendall boy…

BRENDA. No, Rose. Don't you remember he had to go home and change…Harriet is right…It was Raymond Tuttle. He did wet himself.

HARRIET. *(She stands.)* And Mother was dressed as a Fortune Teller, now that I do remember that…she wore a red veil over her face…I'll never forget that.

BRENDA. You're right, a Fortune Teller, I'd forgotten all about that too and Daddy was dressed as a…a cowboy. Oh, now I remember that, Tex the Texas Cowboy… When I asked him why he was dressed like that he said.

(in a deep voice)

'Why Brenda, I'm Tex the Texas cowboy.' I'll never forget that.

(more laughter)

HARRIET. *(slowly shakes her head as she remembers him)* Tex the Texas cowboy… He looked so handsome that night… And that tin star he had pinned to his shirt.

(looks at **BRENDA***)*

He was a Sheriff you know…said he'd always protect us.

(The room falls silent. After a pause **ROSE** *stands and speaks.)*

ROSE. Oh, girls, do you remember that awful Math teacher we had in grade school, Miss Miriam Bender…

HARRIET. Oh, you mean old flash card Bender, 'Now, Harriet, 9 times 7 is what?'…And the look on her face… Who could ever forget her. You know that's why Ester has to balance my checkbook to this day because of her.

BRENDA. *(takes a sip of her drink)* Ester…that's your daughter right? I think Rose mentioned her name.

HARRIET. That's her. Smart as a tack too… I brought some pictures with me, they're in my suitcase…. Would you like to see them?

ROSE. Oh, I would.

BRENDA. We can see them later, can't we?

HARRIET. Now you just wait right here, I'll get them…it's no trouble at all, they're just in the other room.

(She stands and starts to the bedroom then stops and goes back to the table and gets her glass.)

I might have just one more tiny little drink…you know…

BRENDA. Yes, we know, Harriet…

ROSE & BRENDA. *(in unison)* The bus trip.

HARRIET. The bus trip…that's right.

(They laugh.)

You wait right there.

(Then she exits to the kitchen and the bedroom to get her photos.)

ROSE. *(takes a drink and then looks towards* **BRENDA** *whose glass is also empty)* Oh…come on, Brenda let's have just one more, I'm beginning to like vodka I think… Isn't this fun.

(She stands as does **BRENDA.** *)*

BRENDA. Yes, Rose, it is.

(They exit.)

Scene Four

*(Several beats later **HARRIET** enters carrying a small photo album. She sits on the sofa and puts her drink on the table at the front.)*

HARRIET. Come on you two, I have the pictures.

BRENDA. We'll be right in.

(Several beats later they enter with fresh drinks.)

HARRIET. Now you two just sit down.

(She pats the sofa.)

Rose here, Brenda here.

(They sit.)

HARRIET. *(She opens the album.)* Now let me see…oh yes, this is a picture Ester…my daughter you know. Isn't she a pretty thing? Have you ever seen such blue eyes… See that dress she has on, I made it, Homecoming Queen, two years in a row can you believe it?

(She looks at the picture.)

It's just a shame she still had her braces on her teeth… they ruin her smile don't you think…all that metal in her mouth… And this is a picture of…of my Bernard. Wasn't he handsome…my how he spoiled me…he was always there for me you know…until, that is until… Well, anyway here he is standing there in front of Lanes Galore.

ROSE. Oh yes, such a fine looking man.

HARRIET. See how he has is arms around me…that man would never let me go…that's a fact… And that's his partner, standing there to his right, Fred…Fred Wooten. Nicest man in the world…he and his wife Mary go to my church.

(quietly)

He's black you know.

BRENDA. *(looks at her)* So I can see.

ROSE. *(looks up at her, now feeling the drink)* Black is beautiful they say…

BRENDA. *(turns to **ROSE**)* So I've heard, Rose.

ROSE. Who is that, Harriet?

(She points to the picture.)

That man standing there just behind you? My, but he's good looking.

BRENDA. *(moves the book closer to get a better look)* Rose, where? Which man?

ROSE. The one right there.

*(She looks at **HARRIET**.)*

The one Harriet is trying to cover up.

HARRIET. I am not trying to cover it up, Rose…

(She mover here hand.)

ROSE. Oh, yes you are Harriet…look at you.

HARRIET. Oh, for heaven's sake…

(She holds the book out in front of her so they both can see it.)

Here.

BRENDA. Why he is good looking, Rose. Harriet, who did you say that was?

HARRIET. *(quickly changes the topic)* Oh Brenda, do you see that scar, there on Bernard's cheek, his right cheek? Up near his eye?

BRENDA. *(leans closer to the picture)* I think I can, why?

HARRIET. I just remembered something…I'd almost forgotten, do you how he got that…that scar.

*(She looks as if waiting for an answer. **BRENDA** shakes her head.)*

Well, I shouldn't tell you this of course…especially after how I always teased you about…well, he got it from protesting.

(proudly)

HARRIET. *(cont.)* That's right, can you believe it, my Bernard
was a protester… Oh I can still see him standing there
with the others, I was so proud of him. All that push-
ing and shouting…he even held a banner you know.

(*proudly*)

He really did…just think of it, I was married to a radical
just like my sister here. Now, isn't that a small world…

ROSE. *(looks at her)* Gracious, what was he picketing, Harriet?

HARRIET. Piggly Wiggly when they raised the price of beer.

BRENDA. *(She laughs and stands.)* Yes Harriet, that sounds
like just like me…a dedicated protester all right…pick-
eting for cheaper beer.

(*again laughter*)

ROSE. Now Brenda, let's see a picture of your Jeffrey.

BRENDA. Well, I only have a small one, it's in my wallet, I'll
get it later.

ROSE. Nonsense. Now you go right in there and get it, I
would love to see him, wouldn't you Harriet?

(**HARRIET** *nods.*)

BRENDA. Well…let me see if I can find it.

(*She exits to bedroom after several moments she returns
with her wallet and sits down then opens it.*)

It's not very good, maybe you don't want to see it.

(**ROSE** *has her hand out.*)

All right here it is…

(**HARRIET JEAN** *and* **ROSE** *both look.*)

ROSE. Oh…yes, is that him?

HARRIET. Brenda, it's such a dark picture, which one is he?

BRENDA. *(looks to* **HARRIET**, *then points)* The one on the left
Harriet…the one without the dress on. Jeffrey is black.

HARRIET. Oh, I see…

BRENDA. *(nervously)* I said he's black.

ROSE. Yes, I can see that…Such a handsome man…I like his smile.

BRENDA. It was taken the time he took his history class to Washington, D.C. when they visited the Senate Office Building.

HARRIET. In Washington, D.C.? He does look very distinguished, doesn't he, Rose… But who is that woman standing next to your Jeffrey, that can't be a student?

BRENDA. Oh, that…why Harriet, can't you tell, that's me.

HARRIET. *(holds the picture closer then stands)* It is…that's you? You look lovely and…oh my God, just look… Look you are wearing a dress…a real dress, look Rose.

(She hands it to **ROSE** *who also stands.)*

Our Brenda owns a dress.

ROSE. *(looks at it)* Brenda you should always wear dresses, look how lovely you are…you look just like.

(She pauses and stares at the picture.)

BRENDA. Just like who, Rose?

ROSE. *(reaches out and takes the framed picture from the table and gives it to her)* Mother…you look just like Mother.

(She holds up the picture.)

HARRIET. *(looks as well)* Rose is right you know…look at the eyes, the same smile.

(Then she looks at **BRENDA.***)*

You do, you look just like her… Oh, Brenda you should wear a dress more often.

BRENDA. *(stares at the picture)* Oh, I don't look like her…I can't…

ROSE. But you do, you look just like her.

HARRIET. Why can't you, Brenda ? Why can't you look like her?

BRENDA. *(looks up from picture)* Why I just can't, that's all…

ROSE. *(a long pause)* You mean you can't because you don't want to…

BRENDA. That's silly, Rose. Now why wouldn't I want to…

ROSE. I don't think it's silly at all…really I don't.

HARRIET. Everyone does, Brenda, sometimes you can't help it.

BRENDA. (**BRENDA** *turns and looks at her.*) Sometimes you can't help what Harriet?

HARRIET. Why looking like your parents…We all do I suppose, when we grow older…we all begin to look and act like just our parents…Even if we don't want to we do…Ester said she read that in some magazine, how we become our parents. I don't really understand it either, but we do.

(She takes **BRENDA** *hand.)*

But it's all right you know…to look like them.

(She now holds the picture.)

You're like her you know that Brenda, you always were I think. Didn't you ever notice that?…You know how independent she was, you were so much like her… bull headed you might say. Look how she left us…she wanted to prove something to all of us…At least that's how I figured it out, her leaving us and all…she was just proving how independent she was…that she didn't need us, any of us…that she could do it all on her own. Just like you…Oh, I know that probably sounds like nonsense, but still that's how I…

ROSE. Harriet's right you know…She was like that Brenda… stubborn, angry like. We all tried, tried to be what she wanted us to be, but somehow we never measured up to her, did we?…I guess it frightened her, to think that Brenda was just like her and you know you were always her favorite…And as for Harriet.

(She looks at her.)

Well, she knew how much you adored Daddy, how much we all did.

HARRIET. Rose, I only loved him because I couldn't love her, none of us could, she wouldn't let us love her. Remember, how she would always push us away…how she abandoned us…I guess that's why we all loved Daddy so much, because he was so much like us… trapped, just like we were…I guess that's why he drank the way he did, to escape…

BRENDA. *(She nods.)* His drinking…his own way of escaping from himself and her…I guess he was just too weak to face her so he figured that he needed his crutch, his drinks to feel alive…every morning just standing there staring at himself in that bathroom mirror, maybe he just needed something to prove to himself that he was someone…But then to just surrender like that.

(becomes quiet for a few beats)

That's why he left her you know…he gave up…he told me so. Said that he had to get away from her…that he had too before…*(She pauses.)* …before he either killed himself or her.

(She looks at **ROSE** *and then to* **HARRIET** *and quickly put her hand up to her mouth.)*

Oh, my God…I can't believe I said that?…And after I promised him…

(pause)

Do you know that's the first time I have ever told anyone that…that Father had actually threatened someone…I mean it… I never even told that to Jeffrey…never.

HARRIET. But I always thought he loved her…I mean he never spoke up to her, never raised his voice to her… never not that I could recall.

ROSE. But we couldn't speak up to her, you all know that. We couldn't do that, not just leave, not like he did, we were just youngsters then…we couldn't get away from her, run away and just hide…

BRENDA. Oh, you mean like I did, is that what you mean, Rose?

ROSE. For you it was just easier to show your anger by protesting as you called it, Brenda…That's how you got even I guess. You went your own way. You married your

Jeffrey and found out just who you were…for me it was being…well, like Daddy, I guess. Seen and not heard you'd call it. Accept life as it comes. I was afraid to run away… Did you know that? Why, in all the years I was married to Henry, do you know that I never once spoke up to him…never, not even once?

BRENDA. But why, Rose?

ROSE. Remember what Daddy used to say… How you only fight the big battles, never the small ones…well, with Henry we only had small battles. I guess that's why I never had to speak up. None of them were ever worth fighting over.

HARRIET. *(turns and looks at* **ROSE***)* Rose, do you know how I escaped…how I forgot?

ROSE. Do you mean your Pastor and his church?

HARRIET. *(looks at her)* No, Rose…

(Her composure changes ever so slightly.)

Well, not just that…not just Pastor Wilby and his church…

BRENDA. *(looks at* **HARRIET***)* Then how, Harriet?

HARRIET. Bernard…my Bernard, that's how I, how I… When I first saw him that evening in church, well I knew he was the one… He was a plain man really. Not handsome you know…

(wistfully)

But when I saw him standing there by the door… But it was like it had been planned… Like someone had meant for us to meet… I knew that he loved me, I could see it in his face. That he loved me so much that I would never be abandoned, not ever again. Not like she did or Daddy did. He was always there for me just like in that picture…right there beside me always…

ROSE. *(turns to* **BRENDA***)* Brenda, may I ask you something?

(BRENDA *looks at her and nods.)*

ROSE. When we asked to see a picture of your Jeffrey... well...you didn't want us to see it, not at first that is... You didn't want us to know that he was a black man, did you?

(**BRENDA** *continues looking at her.*)

Why? Did it embarrass you? Were you afraid that we would be shocked is that it? That we would not understand...that we might not accept you or maybe dislike him or you?

BRENDA. *(long silence)* Rose when you called me, to ask me here...for this weekend...Well, you know I didn't want to come... I mean I never wanted to... I tried to think of something, anything to tell you just so I wouldn't have to say *yes*...Do you know that?

ROSE. *(nods)* That's just because you were afraid Brenda. Don't you understand that...we all were afraid. Calling that adoption agency was the hardest thing I have ever had to do in my life...and then I was afraid to call you...of going back...of what I might find, what I might hear...of finding what I might not want to find...

BRENDA. I didn't want to have to answer for what I had done...To be judged by you both...I...I was afraid you wouldn't accept me back...as a sister...that I had burned my last bridge all those years ago...

(**BRENDA** *takes* **ROSE** *and gives her a hug.*)

HARRIET. *(leans to* **ROSE** *and hugs her)* Rose, I...I didn't want to come either...to have to face...well to have to face all of this. Mother, Daddy, all of it...I didn't want to be reminded of it, to have to remember that it ever happened to me, that it happened to any of us...I had all of those wonderful years with Bernard to forget, then your call...Then it all came back.

ROSE. *(holding her)* I know Harriet, I know...

BRENDA. Then why Rose, if you knew that...why in God's name did you call us...get us here like this? Make us do this...

ROSE. Because you were worth it, don't you understand…
to me at least you were, both of you were worth it. This
was one battle I had to win, Brenda, can't you see…
that's why I did it, for all of us, for this weekend, for
the Cooley girls. To see my sisters again, that's why… It
just came to me… *'Rose you have to do this, you don't have
a choice. Just stop your accepting and do it'*… I just couldn't
stand by any longer and do nothing, leave things as
they were…not any longer I couldn't. I had two sisters
out there somewhere and I didn't even know where
you were…I had to know…

(Lights slowly fade to black.)

Scene Five

*(It is now Sunday, two days later. The reunion has drawn to a close. As the lights come up we see **ROSE**'s apartment. A piece of luggage sit stage left. **ROSE** and **HARRIET** enter stage right holding coffee cups as the action begins.)*

HARRIET. Dinner was wonderful last night, Rose. Do you know how long it has been since I have had Chinese… well, since Bernard died I suppose? He loved Chinese.

ROSE. I guess the next time I won't try eating Chinese with those little chop-stick things…I just hope the stains will come out of my dress. Dropping all that food in my lap like I did…

*(They both laugh as **BRENDA** enters she to has a cup of coffee.)*

ROSE. Now what time does your bus leave?

*(Looks up and sees **BRENDA** entering. She carries **HAR-RIET**'s book of photographs.)*

Well, here she comes…Harriet and I were just talking about last night…dinner.

*(notices the book of photos as does **HARRIET**)*

HARRIET. *(surprised)* Brenda, what are you doing with my pictures? I had them all packed…

BRENDA. Oh…just taking one last look at them Harriet. You don't mind do you?

HARRIET. Well, that is…why of course not. I brought them for you all to see didn't I?

BRENDA. *(Walks and sits on the sofa. After several beats she looks up at **HARRIET**.)* Harriet…who is Robert?

*(For a moment **HARRIET** says nothing. The question has taken her completely by surprise and she is at a loss to answer)*

BRENDA. Harriet…I asked you…who is…Robert?

HARRIET. *(now becoming nervous and a bit defensive)* Why… why, what do you mean…'Who is Robert?'… What kind of a question is that, Robert who?

BRENDA. Oh, come on Harriet, it's a simple enough question. You remember Friday night when Rose asked you who that man was standing behind you in one of the photos…the good-looking one. Well, you never answered her…so this morning I looked through your book again and found the picture. On the back of it someone had written, 'My dear Robert with us and the Wootens'. I mean someone must have done it. Written his name there…and they are your pictures after all.

HARRIET. What are you saying?…Are you saying that I'm lying? Well, is that it? Well is it, Brenda?

BRENDA. Not lying Harriet, just not telling the truth. Does that sound better?

HARRIET. How dare you…

*(Lunges for the book and grabs it out of **BRENDA**'s hands. **ROSE** takes a step back in shock.)*

How dare you…you…Give me that.

ROSE. *(moves one step towards them)* Now girls…

BRENDA. Rose, I am waiting for an answer here…Now then Harriet, who is Robert?

HARRIET. *(**HARRIET** glares at **BRENDA**.)*

BRENDA. So…you are lying.

*(She looks at **ROSE**.)*

I guess what you were hoping for never really happened then, did it, Rose…this weekend of yours…we haven't changed at all have we. We still have our little secrets, isn't that right girls…secrets.

(She stands and takes several steps to stage right. Then she stops and turns.)

I knew this little get together of yours was flawed, Rose, I knew it from the minute you called me, I swear to God I did… I should have seen it coming.

(She slowly shakes her head.)

BRENDA. *(cont.)* Yet…I fell for it didn't I, wow did I, fell for all of this…

(She sweeps her hands about the room.)

BRENDA. Reunion crap of yours.

(She stands and begins to walk slowly around the apartment as she continues to talk.)

BRENDA. What a sucker I was, I wanted to believe that it was possible…that after all this time… Can you believe it.

(Stops as thought searching for the right word.)

BRENDA. I'll bet you both got a good laugh last night when Brenda, dear old radical Brenda, got a few drinks in her and started spilling out her guts to you two at dinner…am I right? Well, no more, my dear sisters… Do you hear me, no more…That was my last trip under that microscope…you can be damn sure of that. From now on if anyone asks…

(a long beat)

I am an only child.

ROSE. Brenda, don't say that…we weren't laughing. What are you saying…You're mistaken it was nothing like that.

BRENDA. It's too late for that now, Rose, forty years too late.

(She stops and looks at her two sisters.)

I have to tell you two that for a minute there last night I almost bought into what I was saying, what we were all saying to one another. I swear to God, I did. This reunion, to let our hair down, trot out our 'poor little me stories,' get to know each other, bond as though nothing had ever happened, as though we did this meet and greet every god damned summer…just like we were real…real…

ROSE. *(cuts her line)* You mean like we were real sisters again? Is that what you mean Brenda? Well, is it?

BRENDA. *(turns to her and after a pause)* Something like that, Rose.

*(She then turns to **HARRIET**.)*

But Harriet here had other ideas…

*(A long pause as **HARRIET** weighs her words before speaking)*

HARRIET. *(looks to **BRENDA** and then to **ROSE**)* Stop it! Please, just stop it!

(She tries to regain her composure.)

Alright it's Robert…his name is Robert Wilby. That is his name Brenda, the man in the picture. Robert Wilby.

ROSE. *(shocked)* You mean your pastor?

HARRIET. Yes, Rose, my pastor.

BRENDA. *(directly to her now)* He is more then your pastor, isn't he, Harriet? Well, isn't he?

ROSE. Brenda?

BRENDA. *(moves to **HARRIET** now more insistent)* I said, he's more to you then just that isn't he, Harriet? More then you spiritual advisor, isn't that what you called him?

(her tone now flippant)

Your spiritual advisor…Your good pastor.

HARRIET. *(stands motionless for a moment and then shouts out the first word)* Yes…

(Now she continues in almost a whisper.)

Yes…was…was.

BRENDA. I thought you had something to hide…Robert was the man you first saw in church that night wasn't he, Harriet. It wasn't Bernard at all was it, it was this Robert, the one who was going to love and protect you forever…Love at first sight as though it had been planned you said. So it wasn't Bernard was it? It was this, Robert Wilby…Well, wasn't?

HARRIET. *(looks up into* **BRENDA***'s face)* Yes…Yes, it was him… Are you happy now. Is that what you wanted to hear?

(a long pause)

You don't understand…how can you?

(pause)

He was so beautiful, Brenda. And that look…those deep blue eyes of his…the way he…

(Her voice drifts off.)

No one has every looked at me, the way he did that night…or made me feel like I was…

(slowly with emotion)

Someone special… Don't you understand? Don't you know how I felt?

(She looks at the two sisters.)

For the first time in my life I was someone special… me, Harriet Cooley… I was special. And he needed me Brenda, no one ever needed me, not like he did that night…Oh, he was so…

BRENDA. What about Bernard?

HARRIET. What do you mean?

BRENDA. My God Harriet, you married the man, didn't you? Didn't you tell him?

HARRIET. *(She stops and thinks for a moment.)* Bernard was different. He was older, settled, he was my security to hold tight to, but he did love me, truly he did. You do understand that don't you. He loved me. And I needed him, Brenda, I did, I needed someone in my life like Bernard, someone older to love me like…to be like…

(Her voice trails off.)

ROSE. To be like Daddy you mean?

HARRIET. *(She slowly turns to* **ROSE***.)* Yes, Rose, to be like Daddy

BRENDA. And Ester, does she know?

HARRIET. *(Her eyes widen. Her voice controlled)* What about Ester?… Know what?…What are you talking about?

BRENDA. Oh, for Godsake, Harriet, I not pointing any fingers, hell my life not been picture perfect…but all you have to do is look at Robert Wilby's face and then Ester's…you can see it, the resemblance…the blue eyes….

ROSE. *(a gasp)* Oh, Brenda, do you mean?

BRENDA. *(turns to* **ROSE***)* Yes, Rose. That's what I mean.

HARRIET. *(She moves to* **BRENDA** *and takes her by her arms.)* Bernard never knew…I swear to God, he didn't… He always thought that Ester was his child and she was… she was his child.

*(***HARRIET** *moves to sofa and sits.)*

Robert and I…

BRENDA. Have you told Ester?

HARRIET. *(looks at her with a stunned expression)* Told Ester? You mean about…

(She becomes flustered.)

How could I…No, she doesn't know…She'll never know.

ROSE. *(moves to* **HARRIET** *as does* **BRENDA***)* But Harriet, you have to tell her. You just have to.

BRENDA. Rose is right Harriet, she has to know…Christ do you want her growing up not knowing who her real father is…getting a phone call someday like we did from Rose here, is that what you want for her, well is it? Living another goddamned lie for the rest of her life.

ROSE. You can't do that to her, Harriet, not to your own daughter. Look at us, didn't we all live a lie and look what it got us…go ahead, just look at us. Three strangers that call themselves sisters.

HARRIET. *(begins to cry)* But it's been too long, don't you understand? What do I say to her? How can I ever explain? She'll end up hating me I just know it…she will.

BRENDA. *(firmly)* Stop it, do you hear me just stop it... Look Harriet, none of us cared a tinkers-damn about each other until this weekend, we all know that.

(She takes several steps towards stage right and then turns and stops and continues.)

We, just huddled in our own safe little corner...never admitting to a damn thing, thinking we never needed anyone but ourselves...but sometimes you do...

ROSE. Brenda, I think...

BRENDA. *(glances towards* **ROSE***)* No, Rose just let me say what I have to say

(turns to **HARRIET***)*

Harriet needs us, can't you see that, Rose? She needs us. For the first time in our lives we need each other to survive. How can we call ourselves sisters if we just turn our backs on each other now for another forty years? What happened back then just happened, Harriet. Don't you see that, you couldn't help it...but you can't go back now and undo it...run away and try to cover it up with lies. Our choices back then were never up to us...but now they are. Don't you understand that? Now our lives belong to us...Hell, we survived didn't we, that's got to count for something...Now it's up to us to help you and Ester.

HARRIET. *(***HARRIET*** stands.)* But Brenda...I'm...I'm not strong enough to do this on my own, to tell Ester... You know that...I'm not strong enough...I've never been strong...

ROSE. *(***ROSE*** interrupts her.)* But you're not alone Harriett, don't you understand. After forty years none of us will ever be alone again, not like we were back then... We've got each other...We're family now...

BRENDA. *(Cuts her line as she takes* **HARRIET** *in her arms and holds her close as she speaks softly but sternly to her.)* Harriet, you are going to tell Ester the truth...

(pause)

BRENDA. *(cont.)* Do you hear me, *the truth?* Every word of it…Look Harriet, if you love that girl as much as you say you do…then she deserves to hear the truth. Just be honest with her. She'll understand.

*(She pauses for a beat and looks at **ROSE**.)*

And we are going to help you, aren't we, Rose?

*(looks back to **HARRIET**)*

Do you hear me Harriet, Rose and I…your sisters, the Cooley girls are going to help you do it.

*(**HARRIET** begins to cry softly.)*

*(**ROSE** moves to her sisters as they all embrace now)*

(Lights go to black.)

The End

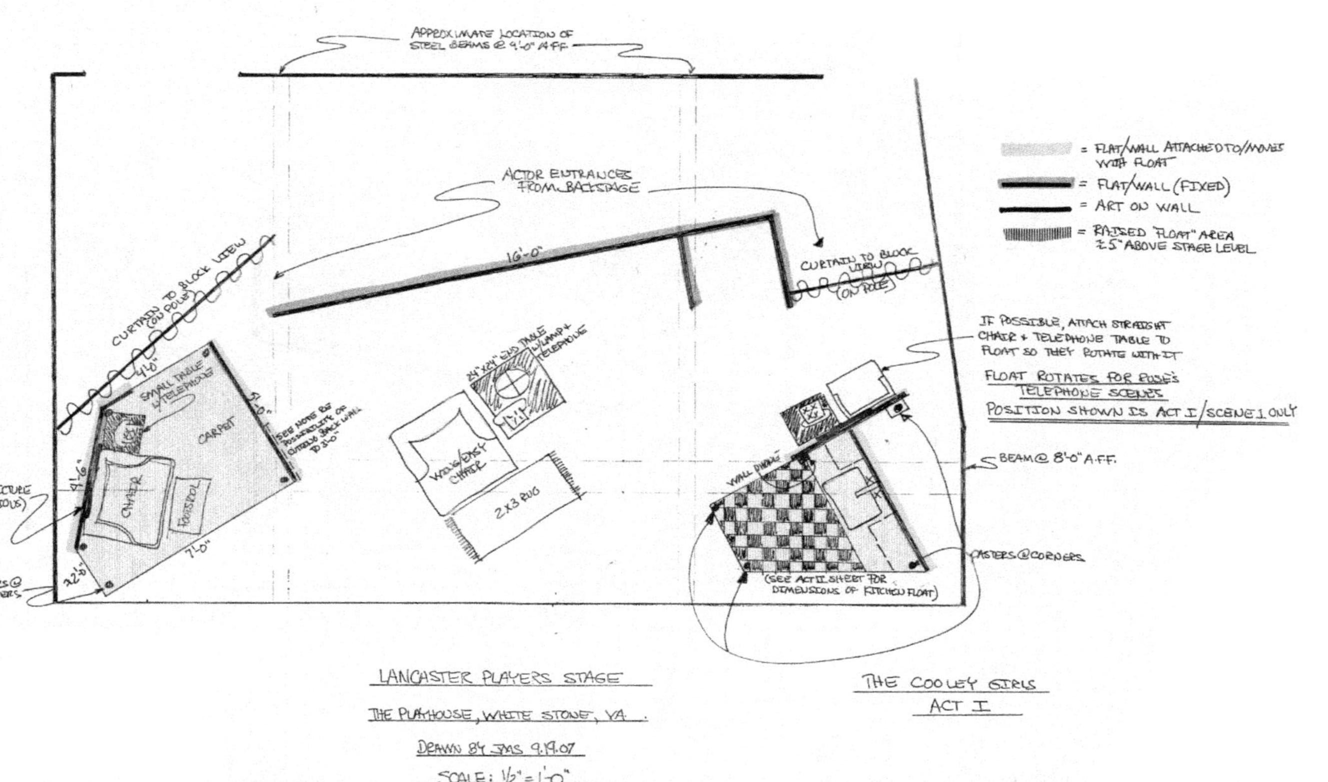

GREEN ROOM
APPROXIMATE LOCATION OF STEEL BEAMS @ 9'-0" A.FF.
= FLAT/WALL ATTACHED TO/MOVES WITH FLOAT
= FLAT/WALL (FIXED)
= ART ON WALL
= RAISED "FLOAT" AREA 2.5" ABOVE STAGE LEVEL
ACTOR ENTRANCES FROM BACKSTAGE
16'-0"
CURTAIN TO BLOCK VIEW (ON POLE)
CURTAIN TO BLOCK VIEW (ON POLE)
IF POSSIBLE, ATTACH STRAIGHT CHAIR & TELEPHONE TABLE TO FLOAT SO THEY ROTATE WITH IT
FLOAT ROTATES FOR ROSE'S TELEPHONE SCENES
POSITION SHOWN IS ACT I / SCENE 1 ONLY
BEAM @ 8'-0" A.FF.
SMALL TABLE W/ TELEPHONE
24"x24" END TABLE W/ LAMP + TELEPHONE
CARPET
SEE NOTE RE: POSSIBILITY OF CUTTING BACK WALL TO 3'-0"
WING/EASY CHAIR
2x3 RUG
WALL PHONE
4'-0"
5'-0"
7'-6"
CHAIR
FOOTSTOOL
7'-0"
22'-0"
WALL PICTURE (RELIGIOUS)
CASTERS @ CORNERS
(SEE ACT II SHEET FOR DIMENSIONS OF KITCHEN FLOAT)
CASTERS @ CORNERS
LANCASTER PLAYERS STAGE
THE PLAYHOUSE, WHITE STONE, VA.
DRAWN BY JMS 9.14.07
SCALE: 1/2"=1'-0"
THE COOLEY GIRLS
ACT I

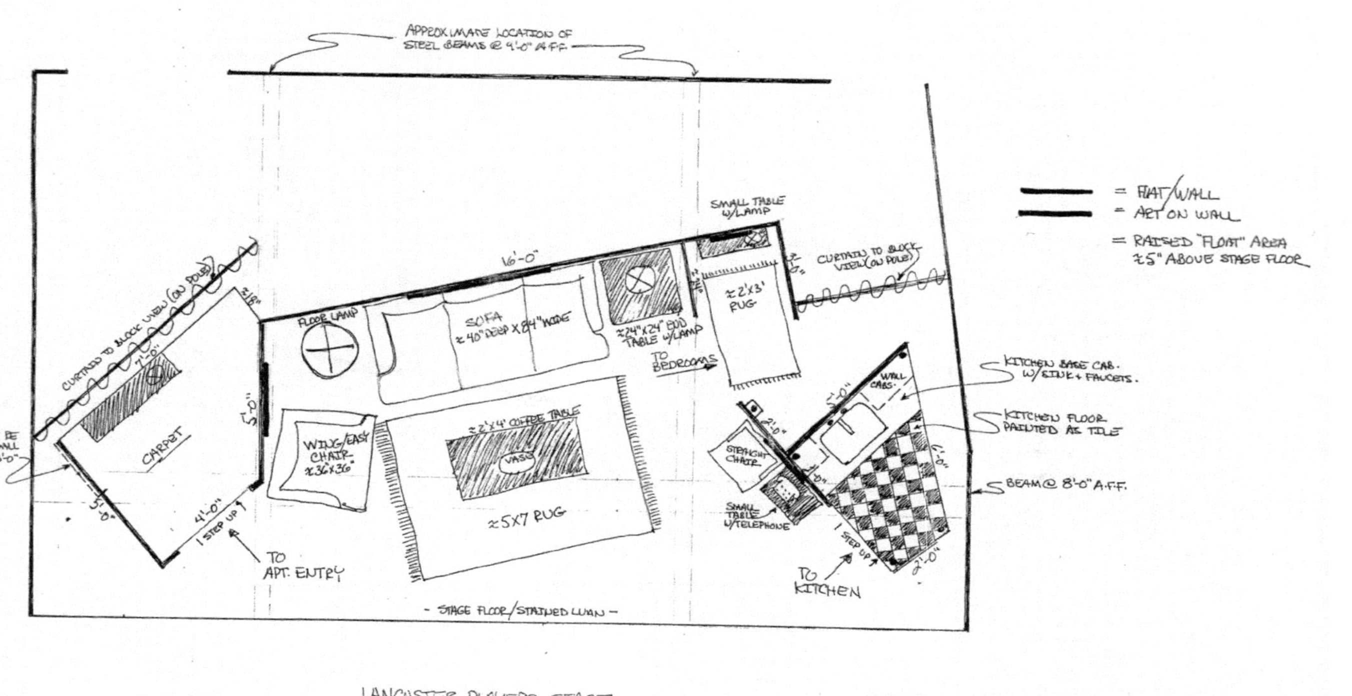
= FLAT/WALL
= ART ON WALL
= RAISED "FLOAT" AREA ±5" ABOVE STAGE FLOOR
GREEN ROOM
APPROXIMATE LOCATION OF STEEL BEAMS @ 4'-0" A.F.F.
CURTAINS TO BLOCK VIEW (ON POLE)
SEE NOTE RE CUTTING WALL BACK TO 8'-0"
CARPET
7'-0"
±18"
5'-0"
5'-0"
4'-0"
1 STEP UP
TO APT. ENTRY
FLOOR LAMP
16'-0"
SOFA ±40"DEEP x 84"WIDE
WING/EASY CHAIR ±36"x36"
±2'x4' COFFEE TABLE
VASE
±5X7 RUG
±24"x24" END TABLE W/LAMP
TO BEDROOMS
SMALL TABLE W/LAMP
±2'x3' RUG
CURTAIN TO BLOCK VIEW (ON POLE)
3'-0"
STAGE FLOOR/STAINED LUAN
KITCHEN BASE CAB. W/SINK + FAUCETS.
KITCHEN FLOOR PAINTED AS TILE
BEAM @ 8'-0" A.F.F.
WALL CABS.
5'-0"
2'-0"
2'-0"
2'-0"
STRAIGHT CHAIR
SMALL TABLE W/TELEPHONE
1 STEP UP
TO KITCHEN
LANCASTER PLAYERS STAGE
THE PLAYHOUSE, WHITE STONE, VA.
THE COOLEY GIRLS
ACT II